Usborne
Sticker Dolly Dressing
Mermaid Kingdom

Written by Fiona Watt

Illustrated by Antonia Miller and Johanna Furst

Contents

Coral reef

Bright sunlight streams through the warm, shallow sea, as the mermaids explore a coral reef. They are fascinated by the strange shapes of the coral and the brightly patterned fish that are swimming around.

Marin

Anemone

Marissa

Underwater city

The mermaids are having fun playing hide-and-seek amongst the ruins of an ancient city. As Galia covers her eyes and counts to twenty, the memaids flick their tails and swim away as fast as they can to find a place to hide.

Galia

Calypso

Mysterious cave

Deep below the surface of the sea, Oriana, Jesper and Celeste are exploring a magical cave. Oriana is delighted to discover an old treasure chest filled with shiny jewels and beautiful seashells.

Oriana

Jesper

Celeste

Tropical lagoon

Turtles love to rest in calm lagoons, safe from the open ocean where waves crash onto the shore. Dragonflies flit and flutter around bright tropical flowers, as elegant fish swim below them.

Ranita

Lula

Alana

Deepsea dance

With arms outstretched, Kaspar and Marilla perform
a graceful dance, far, far below the ocean waves.
Jellyfish gently drift around them, as the mermaids
slowly twist and twirl in the deep, dark water.

Kaspar

Marilla

Royal palace

Carmina is Queen of all mermaids and mermen. She lives in a grand palace, carved into undersea rocks. Her throne is made from gigantic seashells, decorated with pearls collected from oysters that mermaids have discovered on the seabed.

Queen
Carmina

Calista

Kaia

Buried shipwreck

Diving to the seabed, Arion and Maya have discovered
a wooden ship. Arion has found the anchor that was
washed overboard as the ship sank during a raging storm.

Arion

Maya

Seaweed sanctuary

Mermaids love to sit quietly together, surrounded by long strands of swaying seaweed. They share their underwater stories of the sea, as they make pretty necklaces from shiny pearls.

Abalone

Cora

Neri

Crystal

Frozen North

Shafts of green, purple and white light dance across the snowy sky, as Rowan sings to inquisitive seals that have been attracted by her sweet voice. Beneath her, more seals dive and twist with Aria in the icy sea.

Rowan

Aria

Undersea castle

Every year, the Princess of the Sea holds a grand
party in her magnificent underwater castle.
Guided by the flickering lights, magical mermaids,
mermen and other sea creatures join her celebrations.

Syrena

Unicorn island

On warm summer evenings, Delphine and Marina love to swim to the shore and sing while the sun sets. Unicorns, entranced by the beautiful music, canter and leap across the dunes to join them.

Delphine

Marina

23

Seashell slumber

Adina is dreaming of swimming with turtles and diving with dolphins, as she sleeps inside a giant seashell. Seahorses and brightly patterned fish swim by silently, making sure that they don't wake her.

Adina

First published in 2022 by Usborne Publishing Limited, 83-85 Saffron Hill, London EC1N 8RT, United Kingdom. usborne.com
Copyright © 2022 Usborne Publishing Limited. The name Usborne and the Balloon logo are registered Trade marks of Usborne Publishing Limited.